BANDITS HOLLOW

DIANE J. REED

Bandits Ranch Books

This novella is dedicated to all those who love to dance by starlight and wander the world with their hearts open wide.

A deep call echoed through the woods of Bender Lake. It rolled past stark hardwood trees, barren of their leaves on a moonlit winter night, and traveled over the surface of the water till the sound thinned to a low rumble.

Perched high on an oak branch was a great horned owl, chest swelled before its head swiveled full circle. Gold eyes flared as it spied its next prey. Snowflakes that mottled the bird's forehead and feathers made it appear as old and stern as time itself.

Evangeline Tinker stood at the open door of her Traveller's wagon, her long velvet black dress shivering in the cold breeze. She tiptoed to the ground with caution, her laced crimson boots sinking into the soft layer of snow like blood. Wrapping her crocheted shawl tighter around herself, she took a puff on the thin cigar between her teeth, watching its curl of smoke rise to the stars.

"Cold Moon," she muttered under her breath, her gold front tooth gleaming in the moonlight. In her grip was a small leather pouch, the color of turquoise and worn rough and dark at the edges. She scanned the trees around Bender Lake, turning to study the wavy reflection of the full moon on the water like it was her crystal ball, the one she always kept inside her wagon for eager customers. Evangeline Tinker was renowned as the best backwoods fortune teller this side of the Mississippi, though most folks insisted she was the finest anywhere. Legions of pilgrims had made the journey to her wagon over the years, relying on word of mouth to find a remote dirt road past the Turtle Shores Trailer Park, over an hour southeast of Cincinnati. Although she rarely told customers what they wanted to hear.

"Truth hurts, darlin'," she'd remind them in her voice of gravel, whenever they sought answers for their most treasured hopes or fractured love lives. "But it's the only thing that can bring a heart solace." Evangeline's customers left in tears as often as they did with smiles, yet there was always a sense of closure in their eyes—something akin to a hard-won peace—that was worth more to them than money could buy. Even law enforcement had been known to darken Evangeline's door, hoping her psychic abilities might lead them to the remains of bodies long abandoned to cold case files. Sure as the sun sets each evening, Evangeline's peculiar wisdom never failed to disappoint, which often made her a target for underworld types or others who preferred that their secrets remain sealed.

Yet that's where Evangeline Tinker's greatest talent lay.

Expert at gathering herbs and crafting spells in the tradition of her Irish Traveller forebears, Evangeline had an extraordinary knack for knowing how not to be found. Only people whose motives could be trusted ever seemed to locate her. And everyone from Cincinnati, Ohio to Harlan, Kentucky knew their troubles had better be desperate for her to give them the time of day. Most folks attributed her magical elusiveness to the concoctions she mixed only at certain times of year by the light of a full moon. Others claimed it was due to a close-knit group of backwoods militia at the Turtle Shores Trailer Park who guarded their prophetess with a loyalty normally reserved for the historical monarchs of Europe.

But there were some who whispered that it was the moon itself that protected Evangeline...

As Evangeline gazed at the white reflection at the center of Bender Lake, the rays of moonlight that filtered through the trees highlighted her strands of gray hair, full lips and wide cheekbones—features so classically beautiful and arresting that she still took young men's breaths away. All her life, her skin was as pale and smooth as moonstone, and a white streak at her forehead contrasted her dark hair by the time she turned fifteen. Rumors had spread that she'd gone gray due to a lightning strike as a teenager, which she'd survived and had contributed to her other-worldly prescience. Ever since then, Evangeline could be counted on to dash into the woods at midnight every time there was a full moon and whisper while wandering, as though confiding secrets to her lunar best friend.

"If'n the moon shines like a silver shield," she recited the old folklore rhyme, "ya needn't be afraid to reap yer fields." Evangeline nodded at the pouch in her hand and bent down to pick up a frosted branch from the ground. "Mighty good night fer diggin' my roots."

The great horned owl bellowed again, its hoot piercing the woods with a series of echoes before the sound fanned out across the lake like an eerie summons. For the life of her, Evangeline could've sworn she heard one of the echoes call her name.

A chill began to work its way down her spine.

"Dammit!" A woman's voice cursed abruptly in the darkness, distracting Evangeline's train of thought.

Evangeline spotted her friend Brandi in the distance between the trees, grumbling as she hopped down from her vintage Airstream trailer that glowed with a hundred Christmas lights, casting a kaleidoscope of red and green onto the snow. Brandi slammed her door so hard that her trailer shook, and she stomped toward the source of the owl's noise with her fists tight. She wore a curious outfit for such a late hour, sheathed in a leopard-print jumpsuit and matching kitten heels, and she had on a surprising amount of makeup, complete with bright purple lipstick and false eyelashes. As Brandi marched doggedly through the woods on teetering heels that kept slipping sideways, she didn't appear to notice Evangeline in the moonlight until she was nearly on top of her.

"Lord have mercy!" Brandi gasped when she spied Evangeline's crimson boots in the snow. She glanced up with a start at Evangeline's moonlit face. "Granny Tinker, what the hell are you doing up at this hour?"

"Same as you, I reckon." Evangeline rolled her cigar to the corner of her mouth and nodded at the owl above them before releasing another puff. For a moment, the smoke obscured her face entirely.

Brandi coughed and waved the cloud aside, all the more

irritated. "Well I swear, how's a body supposed to get any sleep 'round here with that damn owl's racket!" Hands on her hips, she shook her head sharply, causing one of her false eyelashes to flutter down her cheek and tumble to the snow.

Evangeline merely smiled. She knew Brandi's dark moods never lasted long, given her ebullient personality. "Is there a reason yer dressed like Anne Margaret from one of them old Las Vegas movies?" she chuckled, swinging her turquoise pouch back and forth.

Brandi scanned her curve-hugging, leopard-print jumpsuit and sighed. "Aw hell, I just got back from my shift at the Moo & Brew Drive Thru fifteen minutes ago. Ol' Charlie has us working late during the holiday season so folks can get their eggnog whenever they want." Brandi gave Evangeline a sly wink. "Shh, don't tell nobody, but he sells his moonshine on the side to give it a kick. Folks give me pretty good tips when I wear these outfits and pour a little extra into their cartons."

"Now when have *I* ever been known to talk too much?" Evangeline replied.

Brandi blushed. It was common knowledge that it would be easier to pry a liar's soul out of Satan's clutches than to ever wrestle a secret from Evangeline. She swallowed hard and backpedaled quickly.

"I dare say though," Brandi remarked with sincerity in her eyes, "this moonlight does do wonders for your complexion. You look younger all of a sudden, sweetie. Must be the shiny silver light. You know, I've always thought about dying my hair with streaks of platinum like yours. Might get me more tips—"

Brandi's words were cut short by the silent thrust of air from a pair of wings that soared mere inches above their heads, startling them both. A crinkled piece of paper fluttered to the ground, and as the owl passed over them to the woods, its moon shadow stretched over the snow.

Only it wasn't the silhouette of a bird...

It was the shadow of a *man*.

"Looky-look!" Brandi squealed, oblivious, pointing at the ground. "That owl dropped a piece of paper!" She scooped it up and unraveled the note in her hands, noticing it was yellowed and stained at the edges like old parchment.

"Why, it's a poem!" she marveled, scanning the faded words written in a florid script, the way penmanship used to look in the nineteenth century. "Heavens, it's lovely," Brandi sighed. "You gotta listen to this, sweetie," she urged as she read the note aloud:

> I was young once, too
> in the wood and the hollow
> where magic seeks you
> and your steps must follow.
> Your heart was open then,
> and will be again,
> for I will find you
> *and this isn't the end...*

"Land sakes! That's by *far* the most romantic thing I've ever heard!" Brandi gushed, searching Evangeline's eyes. "You never told me you had a paramour! And a poet, no less, with a trained owl for a messenger! C'mon now, cough it up—is he tall, dark and handsome, or what?"

To Brandi's bewilderment, Evangeline's face drained of all

color. Her timberwolf gray eyes with golden flecks in the middle, the kind that always seemed to see to eternity and back, became strangely dimmed of light. For a woman who prided herself on not being found when she didn't want to be, it was the first time Brandi had ever seen a hint of fear in Evangeline's expression. Let alone what looked like raw terror.

Evangeline gripped Brandi's shoulder so tightly that she flinched and tried to pull away, to no avail.

"Run, Brandi," Evangeline insisted in a hoarse voice, as if her breath had been knocked out of her.

She grabbed the poem from Brandi's hands and threw it against the snow like a piece of hot coal she couldn't bear to hold. Evangeline pointed a trembling finger at a set of peculiar hoof tracks near her wagon, which looked like a mysterious rider had visited briefly and then simply disappeared. When she returned her grip to Brandi's shoulder, she gave her a hard shake.

"In the name of everythin' you hold dear," Evangeline urged, "run Brandi, for your ever lovin' life."

Evangeline released her and ripped open the cuff from the sleeve of her black velvet dress, threads dangling in the moonlight. An old scar was visible on the inside of her pale forearm that read *Virgil*, followed by hash marks beneath it, tracking some kind of score.

"Go, I said!" Evangeline repeated to Brandi, who seemed scared witless, her feet immobile in the snow. "Go before he marks yer soul."

2

E vangeline ground her cigar onto the note in the snow, where it burned a hole in the poem and snuffed out with a hiss. She hoisted up her velvet dress and began to race, leaving Brandi, her wagon, her friends at Bender Lake and her whole life behind. Clutching her turquoise pouch with a death grip, her eyes were focused on a narrow, snowy path that was barely visible in the woods, which wove past scraggly, leafless honeysuckle bushes. Branches whipped at her legs, arms, and cheeks as she tore through the forest, glancing up every few strides at the position of the moon like it was her compass. Her muscles groaned and her lungs felt as if they were ready to melt, yet she lunged forward, faster and faster, like a woman who believed time was running out.

Because it was…

Searching desperately for a small creek on the west side of the lake, she finally spied the white domes of snow that capped the rocks along the banks, making them look like a row of mushrooms in the moonlight. Beside them was a shadow, standing nearly as tall as her wagon and darker than anything in the forest.

She *knew* the outline of that silhouette. That soul—

Evangeline halted in her tracks.

"Heard the call, did ya, darlin'?"

The shadow turned to peer at the old trailers and cabins behind her, deep in the woods of Bender Lake, sparkling with blinking holiday lights.

"Merry Christmas—"

Evangeline thrust her pouch up high, the way some vampire seekers raise a silver cross. She fumbled to open the pouch and dug her fingers inside, withdrawing a pinch of dark herbs. Spinning on her heels, she sprinkled them around her until the snow looked like it had been peppered with gunpowder.

"Ain't no magic on this earth can keep me away from what's mine," the shadow merely laughed.

With every word he spoke, his outline became more three-dimensional, as if every beat of Evangeline's racing heart only served to make him more real. Soon, before her stood a man over six feet tall in a long black duster, flanked at the shoulders with buffalo hide, his rugged features framed by silver hair. All around him were horse prints that had trampled in the snow, but led nowhere, as if the horse had somehow dropped from the sky and then vanished.

"I let Spook go back," he smiled, nodding at the way Evangeline's eyes searched the tracks in confusion. "You remember my dappled gray mare? Finest getaway horse in the West—"

"Y-You're old, Virgil Hollow. Y-You sh-should be dead."

Virgil fingered the silver stubble on his chin and smiled, making him appear even more handsome and distinguished than Evangeline had dared to remember. Hot prickles skittered along her cheeks and neck, seeping down her back toward places she'd rather not name. This was the only man on earth who'd ever touched—no, stroked and set afire—every inch of her, igniting her whole body with a desire that would gladly pursue her for centuries. But the only problem was, he should have passed away a hundred years ago.

"H-how, can you be here, Virgil?"

"How could you go *there*, to Colorado way back then? These things are mysterious, ain't they, darlin'?"

Virgil pulled out a hand-rolled cigarette from his duster and struck a match, cupping his hand to light it and tossing the match into the trickling creek beside him. Rather than smolder as it hit the water, a plume of fire rose up, as though ignited by vapors. It illuminated Virgil's sharp, weathered features, toughened by years of living outdoors on the frontier—and on the run.

"You know, you never told me when you reclined on my Indian blankets and buffalo hides at night, running your fingers over my skin by moonlight in my hideout, that you were from another century. One from the future." He glanced her up and down with a glint in his eye. "The way you dress, Evangeline, you could pass as a Victorian lady any day. And you're every bit as beautiful as I remember. Maybe more so—"

Virgil's sly smile, with a grin that flashed mischievous in the moonlight, was enough to send Evangeline's heart aflutter all over again. She *hated* that feeling—the loss of control, the vulnerability that had no bottom to it. The way every pulse of her being might start to crave him once more, enough to drive any sane woman batty. *No one with a lick o' sense loses her heart to a highwayman who robs trains an' stagecoaches*, she thought, *even if he does claim to do it for noble reasons.*

Shaking her head, Evangeline closed her shawl around herself tightly as though trying to seal off her heart as well. She dipped her chin to nod at him out of courtesy and faked a smile, gazing into those blue eyes of his that could drown a woman's heart faster than the depths of Bender Lake. Then she gathered her dress at the hips to give him a polite curtsy, the way she figured Victorian ladies do, while secretly fishing out the switchblade from her dress pocket and hiding it in her palm. Evangeline smiled, revealing the familiar gold front tooth that he recognized and secretly loved her for. Virgil always said it made her look like a pirate's woman, befitting an outlaw like him. Then quick as a flash, she dashed deeper into the woods, coursing down hidden deer paths that only she knew, and out of Virgil's sight.

Unfortunately, she'd forgotten that swiftness was the very reason Virgil succeeded so wildly as a bandit. Within a few strides, he easily caught up with her and scooped her into his arms so fast that it made her head spin.

And in his fist, he had a hold of her switchblade, too.

"You gonna cut me?" Virgil hissed bitterly. "Any deeper than you already have?"

His lips were mere inches away from Evangeline's, so close that she could smell the hand-grown tobacco on his breath from the cigarette he'd dropped by the gaseous creek. "You made me love you, woman," he whispered. "And then you bolted, taking my heart with you…for centuries. That's what I call stealin', Evangeline. And where I come from, it's a crime. A crime that has to be paid for—"

"It warn't my fault!" Evangeline fought back, kicking and wriggling fiercely to grab at her switchblade. "I couldn't help it you fell fer me. You're *crazy*—"

The irony of that word was not lost on her. As soon as she uttered it, she sank in regret, watching the way it made Virgil tilt his head back and laugh.

"No," he replied in a low tone that sounded like it came straight from his soul, "I'm *not* crazy." He smiled, clutching her body tighter to his chest and relishing the feel of her warmth and weight in his arms, along with the fight in her eyes. "And you hate that all to hell about me," he observed, eyes dancing. "That's exactly what you never betted on. That somewhere in this old world, there might actually be some cowboy strong enough to withstand the Tinker curse that drives men mad. Even if I did live over a hundred years ago. But you were never a very good fit for this century, now were you, darlin'?"

Virgil absorbed Evangeline in a kiss, and in spite of her struggle, the scent of pinion pine, gunpowder, and campfire smoke from his life on the run enveloped her, making memories of her dalliance with him in the wilderness of Colorado come rushing back. Thoughts Evangeline had tried to get rid of for decades, to numb with spells, potions, alcohol —anything that might help her release the lingering allure of Virgil Hollow. She'd buried herself in the demanding problems of her customers at Bender Lake for ages, but then that damn owl beneath a Cold Moon had called to her outside her wagon, just like it did all those years ago when she'd gone herb hunting and fell back in time into Virgil's arms. What special magic had been used to draw her? She gripped the turquoise pouch fiercely in her hand.

She knew the answer…

Inside that pouch was the medicine of a man who was even more powerful than her Irish Traveller ancestors.

Iron Feather.

He was a Native American friend of Virgil's. Part Ute, part Apache, and part nobody knew what. He belonged to no tribe but was welcomed by many, except for the Comanche, and he sometimes ran with the Bandits Hollow Gang. Whenever he felt like it.

Yet they were soul brothers, Iron Feather and Virgil Hollow. Knotted hearts, coming from different ways of life and people entirely, after Virgil had saved Iron Feather's life in a shoot out. Nothing seemed to scare those two, no law could rein them in—and they'd do anything for each other.

Even call forth the one woman who was strong enough to be Virgil's lover from a future century?

Virgil drowned Evangeline in another kiss. As she felt herself falling, falling into the pursuit of his lips, all at once she realized he had more than her trusty switchblade in his hand. He'd snagged her turquoise pouch as well. Or rather, *his* pouch —the one Iron Feather had given him to protect him whenever he was away.

"Iron Feather's gone now, Evangeline," Virgil said in a solemn tone as his lips broke from hers. He held up the old pouch to her face, swinging like a pendulum on a chain, and pulled it away from her each time she tried to seize it. "His spirit's calling his medicine back to him. This medicine that protected me and you, and everyone it was passed to." He studied its turquoise color for a moment. "It must go back to his side."

Virgil gazed into Evangeline's eyes like *she* was the real medicine he'd been searching for all this time. "But as long as I have you," he glanced up at the Cold Moon for a few seconds as if for courage, "I'm willing to give luck another try." He began to walk with her in his arms back to the creek of vapors. "We're going now, Evangeline."

"No!" cried Evangeline, attempting to wrestle her fists from the strength of his bear grip. But Virgil's strides were long and lanky, and they were beside the creek in no time. Waiting for them in the shadows, however, was something Virgil hadn't counted on—

It was subtle, a mere click in the darkness that piqued Virgil's and Evangeline's attention. But both of them heard it as loud as a blast from a cannon. There was no mistaking the sound of cocking a revolver.

"You ain't goin' nowhere, mister!" a voice cut through shadows. "And you can put Granny Tinker down this instant."

Brandi emerged from the darkness, her trembling gun aimed straight at Virgil Hollow's head. "Forgive me Granny," she said. "I know you don't allow firearms nowhere near Turtle Shores, but I've had this one in secret from a long time ago, just in case one of your potions fails, if you know what I mean. And from the looks of it," Brandi glared at the handsome, weathered face of Virgil with Evangeline's pouch in his hand, "this might be one of those moments."

Virgil grinned, infuriating Brandi.

"You take one more step, mister, and I swear I'll blow your head clean off," Brandi hissed, both hands on the weapon now. She closed one eye and stared down the barrel. "Evangeline's the best goddamn friend I ever had in this world—the best most anybody's ever had—and I'll die before I'll let anything happen to her."

Though her heart was racing a mile a minute, it was the first time Evangeline had ever heard such cold words coming from Brandi's glossy purple lips. Brandi's eyes squinted into thin lines, and Evangeline could tell she meant business. Nevertheless, despite Evangeline's efforts to kick madly and elbow Virgil in the face, his big arms clutched her thin frame harder as he stepped closer to the creek.

"Stop! Stop, I said!" Brandi demanded. "Duck, Granny!"

Brandi pulled the trigger and fired at Virgil—

The bullet sailed through the apparition of his head, which had become hazy the moment he stepped into the creek, ricocheting off a tree behind him.

Lowering her weapon in shock, Brandi watched in horror as Virgil and Evangeline became wavy, as though lost in a vapor, and then disappeared.

3

"I don't know how to explain it," Brandi moaned, burying her head in her hands.

She was sitting in her friend Lorraine's trailer as Lorraine was whipping up a breakfast of hot cakes for her neighbors at the Turtles Shores Trailer Park. She'd dyed the batter green with food coloring, and each hot cake was in the shape of a Christmas tree that she created by ladling the batter onto her griddle just right. Then she stacked them in neat piles on a plate at the side of her stove, until her neighbors' noses made them follow the divine scent of bacon and hand-harvested maple syrup to her door.

"Are you tryin' to tell me that Granny up an' disappeared?" Lorraine shook her head, pausing with a spatula in her hand. "Honey, I've heard a hell of a lot of strange things about Bender Lake in my day. Sasquatch sightings, alien abductions, fairy troops on the warpath, not to mention a few dark personages who take revenge by dumping bodies here. But I gotta say, this one takes the damn cake."

"It's true!" Brandi lifted her fingers from her face, her expression sunken. "I watched with my own eyes as Granny and this handsome stranger stepped inside a creek in the woods. They plain vanished! You think Bender Lake has got some kind of sinkhole or mystical vortex going on? How could my bullet float right through that son of a bitch?"

Brandi reached toward Lorraine's griddle to warm her hands, checking her glossy, leopard-print nails before searching her friend's face.

Lorraine bit her lip. Her countenance appeared oddly blanched. "You know, folks back in the hollers used to call them things burnin' springs. But I never knew whether to believe 'em or not."

"Burnin' what?"

"Springs," Lorraine repeated. "Hot spots. Cracks in the earth where some kind of vapor gets released over a natural spring. They can make the air look real eerie at night. You heard the term great balls o' fire?"

Brandi nodded slowly.

"Well, that's where the sayin' comes from. Burnin' springs release gasses they say, and in the moonlight they can make different colors hover over a creek or swampy spot in the woods. But then…"

"Then what?" pushed Brandi. She swiped a Christmas tree hot cake from the stove and bit off the top, chewing impatiently while she waited for Lorraine to answer.

"Well, you might think this is kind of crazy," Lorraine said cautiously, "but Granny always told me that's where haints like to linger. Maybe it's magical somehow."

Brandi ceased chewing. She laid her half-eaten hot cake next to the pile of Christmas trees at the edge of Lorraine's stove and cleared her throat. "A-Are you tryin' to tell me that the fella that grabbed Granny was a—"

"Ghost!"

The sound of little Dooley's voice at the entrance to Lorraine's trailer made the two women jump. A tow-headed, six-year-old boy grinned at their reaction and reached over to Lorraine's stove to steal a Christmas tree hot cake, stuffing it greedily into his mouth. Beaming, he held up a square mirror with an antique frame that he'd brought over from Granny's wagon, the one she always said came from her great-great grandmother in Ireland.

Brandi studied the mirror in his hands. "You been out tryin' to catch badgers again?" she asked her sometimes foster child, who had a habit of being parented by virtually everyone in Turtle Shores Trailer Park ever since his mother Caroline passed away. Brandi rolled her eyes and glanced at Lorraine. "Granny told Dooley that badgers are vain and love to see their reflections, whether in a pond or a lake, so when you hold up a mirror to their holes, they come right out to take a look. Then ya nab 'em."

"Me an' Bixby caught two this month!" Dooley beamed. "Remember?" You had 'em in Lorraine's stew, an' Bixby already sold the skins to a feller on Boxcar Road."

A green pallor overcame Brandi's face, and she turned to Lorraine with pursed lips. But rather than scold her for cooking up badger without telling anyone that's what they'd been eating, she merely sighed.

"Listen, it's back to business," Brandi said in a serious tone. "Dooley, did Granny ever tell you she could see haints in her mirror?"

Dooley was about to reply when Lorraine piped up. "Everybody knows you can't see spooks in a mirror. They ain't got no souls—"

"Granny can!" Dooley nodded with pride. "She can see everything. And she said haints *do* have souls—that's why they're so dang confused and still runnin' around. When I was visiting her wagon once, she pointed 'em out to me. A couple a ghosts passed right by her mirror while we were playin' checkers."

The sound of an explosion rocked Lorraine's trailer, making Brandi leap down the steps to where Dooley stood to grab the mirror in his hands before he dropped and broke it.

"Dammit!" Brandi called out to the silhouettes of two men who dashed between the trees. Their round figures appeared to be wearing boulder costumes for camouflage. "How many times do I got to tell you TNT Twins not to blast out badgers from their holes? That ain't no way to find a pet. Or meat, I reckon."

When Brandi held up the mirror to check if it had gotten cracked, she saw something flitter past a corner of the glass.

"L-Lorraine," she said to her friend. "D-didn't you tell me once that your mama liked to wear a red coat around Christmas time?"

"Yes ma'am," Lorraine replied, pouring maple syrup from a ceramic jug into a pot on her stove to warm it. "It was made out of bright red wool, the fanciest piece of clothing she ever had. But she passed on twenty years ago last Christmas Eve."

Brandi glanced Dooley's way, who was scampering off to join the two men in the woods in boulder costumes with sticks of explosives in their hands. She checked the mirror in her grip again.

"Well, she's here visiting you now," Brandi nodded, her face appearing pale. "And somethin' tells me if we want to find out what happened to Granny, we're gonna have to use her heirloom mirror."

4

Brandi trudged through the woods of Bender Lake with the antique mirror in one hand and the other clasped tightly around Lorraine's. Since it was her day off from the Moo & Brew, Brandi wore heavy boots lined with fur and more appropriate winter clothing, given the December weather. She led Lorraine carefully to where the creek was that she'd seen the night before under the Cold Moon. Both women were bundled in wool coats and scarves, with hats, mittens, and earmuffs to keep them warm. After all, neither knew how long it might take to see what happened to Granny, and in the satchel Lorraine carried was some wood in case they decided to build a fire.

Brandi's coat pocket held her revolver as well. It hadn't been much help the night before, but she wasn't going to place any bets that it might not come in handy.

Breathing so hard that puffs of moisture escaped her lips, Brandi set down the old mirror beside the creek. She happened to notice there was a perfect line of round stones beside it, covered with tufts of snow like glistening mushrooms.

"Do ya think somebody marked this place as where a burnin' spring might be?"

"Reckon it was Granny herself," Lorraine replied. "She always came out here to collect roots and herbs, come rain, sleet, or hail, even if she had to dig for 'em with gloves on in the snow. She said they grew best here, near this spot, 'cause that's where the departed came to bless 'em."

"Departed?"

"Yep. I think she believed her Traveller ancestors helped infuse the herbs with power."

"Well, she always could heal about anything that pained a person," Brandi nodded. "So let's go to work."

Brandi propped up the mirror against a tree next to the line of stones and rolled a couple of nearby rocks in front of it to help keep it vertical. Then she grabbed Lorraine's hand and stepped back to look directly in the mirror.

"So what do we do now? Chant somethin' to see what happened to Granny?"

Lorraine shrugged. She folded her arms for a moment and thought about it, tapping her lip. "You know, I seem to recall her sayin' once that if'n you ask properly, a spirit is obliged to show itself and speak. But who's to say what 'proper' is to a spook?"

"Polite words, I expect. Here," Brandi grasped Lorraine's hand again, "let's give it a try." She looked intently into the mirror. "Granny, we know this mirror can show us that spirit that whisked you away. So if you don't mind—"

"Stop," Lorraine halted Brandi. "That ain't her real

name. She don't have no grandchildren I know of. She just goes by the name Granny 'cause a lot of folks don't like to give their real names around Bender Lake. You know, 'cause of their—"

"Pasts?" Brandi finished. "Especially a woman like Granny, right? Who some bad folks would love to see dead. Then what do you think is her real name?"

Lorraine shook her head. "God as my witness, I don't know. She never would reveal it to anybody, and compromise their safety if someone came lookin' for her. But I saw an E once embroidered on one of her pillows in her wagon. Maybe it's for Evelyn? Or Eileen, or—"

"Evangeline."

A voice whispered through the morning mist, startling Brandi and Lorraine. Inside the mirror, from within the reflection of the early fog around Bender Lake, a woman appeared.

She had bright red hair which tumbled in wild curls to her shoulders. A streak of gray swept across her forehead, like Granny's, and she was wearing a long, dark skirt with an apron, cinched tightly at the waist, and a shawl over her head and shoulders that looked like a cape. Yet at the bottom of her skirt, her feet were bare and slightly soiled. She stood next to a bohemian wagon with an old draft horse hitched to it, her head held high and her eyes fiercely focused, with that same timberwolf gray that gave everyone who knew Granny Tinker the shivers.

"Evangeline," the woman whispered again as if from beyond the grave. Brandi and Lorraine grabbed a hold of each other, their bodies riddled with goosebumps. To their confusion, the woman smiled slightly, and she turned to gesture at what appeared to be mist behind her.

"Do you think that's Granny's great-great grandma? The one who passed down the mirror?" Brandi whispered to Lorraine.

"F-From the sound of her talkin', I'd say that's right," Lorraine stuttered. "They both have the same kind of voice."

"And *eyes*," Brandi nodded. "I guess Granny's real name must be Evangeline. So pretty—it's a shame she could never use it." Brandi paused, swallowing hard. "Her great-great grandma is trying to show us something in the mist, Lorraine. I figure it's what happened to Evangeline. You ready?"

"No," Lorraine replied, trembling. She sighed. "But I reckon it ain't up to me."

Brandi hugged Lorraine tighter and gave the woman in the mirror a timid nod. "Can you please help us find our f-friend," she asked kindly, assuming that's how one addresses a spirit.

"There will be a price," the woman answered with an Irish lilt.

"W-what kind of price?" Lorraine inquired, her shoulders trembling.

The woman smiled again, her twinkling eyes the only thing that shined from her peasant demeanor.

"Now when does a Traveller woman ever reveal her secrets?"

5

Brandi turned to Lorraine and searched her face, but Lorraine's eyes were downcast, lost in thought.

"I don't think Evangeline wanted to go with that man willingly," Brandi observed. "So I'm not sure we have much choice. We gotta help her somehow, price or no price."

Lorraine nodded. "Then let's get on with it."

Brandi drew in a deep breath and called out to the woman in the mist. "Please show us where Evangeline went, and how we can get her back."

The woman stepped aside in the mirror and the mist began to thin. Soon, instead of hardwood trees, stripped of their leaves around Bender Lake, before them a pine forest appeared with snow-capped mountains in the distance, lit by the light of a full moon that made the blanket of snow shine like stars. On a branch, a great horned owl lifted its wide wings and hooted, flashing its gray and white feathers to the moon.

And there was Evangeline Tinker, who Brandi and

Lorraine only knew as an older woman, now young and perhaps in her twenties. It was dark outside and she was in the forest, walking alone in one of her typical, velvet dresses and the same crimson, lace-up boots, scanning the snowy bases of trees and old logs with a lantern in her hand. Every once in a while, she'd pull out a small, empty jar from her pocket and sigh, shaking her head. A voice cut through the air from Evangeline's great-great grandmother.

"I passed down all the herbs and plants I'd dried in my lifetime to my descendants," she noted with an Irish cadence to her voice. "But by the time Evangeline was a woman, some of the herbs had run out. The most magical ones, of course. And the problem was that they'd become extinct."

Brandi's brow furrowed, not understanding at all what this had to do with Evangeline's disappearance in the creek. Then in the mirror, she could see an image of Evangeline sprinkling what herbs she did have remaining from another vial. Her lips were moving, speaking some kind of incantation, and she held out her arms to the moon. All at once, she disappeared—

Brandi gasped, only to hear Evangeline's great-great grandmother describe what happened.

"Evangeline came up with a unique solution that day," she noted. "She cast a spell that she thought would help her find the right herbs. And it did—by taking her back in time over a hundred years. She was transported to a remote area in Colorado in the late 1800s. She didn't know that's where she was headed, of course. She only asked the powers that be to send her to where the herbs could be found. But that also sent her straight into the arms of Virgil Hollow."

And sure enough, in the mirror, there was Virgil Hollow,

too. He was a young man, then, with hair as black as anthracite and riding a dappled gray horse, waiting for his partner to toss a bag of money from a stagecoach they were holding up. But along with receiving the bag, Virgil found his open arms also catching Evangeline Tinker, who'd dropped from the sky.

"Love happens that way sometimes," Evangeline's great-great grandmother appeared in the mirror with a slight smile. "Out of the blue, when you least expect it."

"But I thought there was a Tinker curse," piped up Lorraine. "Evangeline told me once she never allows herself to be attracted to any man, 'cause the Tinker women drive men mad. Not angry, but crazy—the kind o' crazy that howls at the moon each night and tries to follow the Tinker women's scent through farm and field, hoping to catch a glimpse of 'em. Evangeline said her life had been littered with dozens of poor souls who'd ended up in straight jackets, babbling to nobody."

"Evangeline is not inclined to tell everything she knows," her great-great grandmother replied. Strangely, she began to disappear. All at once, they saw Evangeline in the arms of Virgil Hollow on his gray mare as he attempted to make a getaway from the stagecoach. He'd fired a couple of shots into the air when he stared, wild-eyed, at the beautiful young woman on his saddle, between him and a bag of cash.

"W-Where'd you come from?" Virgil stuttered, aghast, never slowing his horse's gallop for a second. He wrapped his arms around Evangeline and fired one last shot back at the stagecoach driver for good measure. "Did you jump from the coach? Sweetheart, we're hardly the kind of men a decent lady should be seen with—"

"That's all right, 'cause decent is about the *last* thing I've ever been called," Evangeline replied, laughing. She swiveled in Virgil's lap to face the front of the saddle and grabbed the reins from his hands, giving the horse a kick. "By the way," she turned to call back to him, her voice stolen by the wind, "got any herbs?"

6

"The only one who has herbs around here is Iron Feather," Virgil said, his striking face lit with the orange and red hues by a campfire. "He keeps 'em in his pouch."

Virgil nodded at one of the three outlaws sitting on logs around the fire with him who had a turquoise pouch dangling from a rawhide string in his hand. He was a Native American man in his late twenties, like Virgil, with long black hair that swept to his shoulders. He wore a dark, flat-brimmed hat, the kind many Native American men used to wear in the Southwest, and he had on a black wool coat with brass buttons over deerskin pants and moccasins. Iron Feather's fingers traced over the bulge of his pouch as he met Evangeline's gaze. Dancing flames reflected in his dark eyes.

"This medicine is powerful," he warned, tapping his fingers on the pouch. "It holds more than you know. But you must earn it."

"Aw, now hold on," one of the outlaws said, a scruffy young man with blonde curls who looked like he hadn't bathed in weeks. "You ain't hinting that she's gonna ride with the Bandits Hollow Gang, are ya? We don't have use for a woman 'round here—"

Iron Feather held up a revolver to cut the man off.

It worked. The camp became eerily silent, but for the crackling sound of wood on the fire.

"We have use for her *magic*," Iron Feather insisted. He nodded at Evangeline. "You see things. True?"

Evangeline, her face unlined and dewy in her twenties, yet with eyes as cunning as a wolf's, nevertheless lost any measure of color in her cheeks. All along, she'd thought she was in control. On a lark, merely heading into the woods to collect supplies and casting what she'd thought was an ordinary spell to replenish her herbs. So she happened to land in Colorado around the year 1895, which she surmised from the type of stagecoach they'd robbed. But surely she could cast a spell to return as easily as she'd come, right? She'd heard stories growing up about how her great-great grandmother traversed through time at a whim, always winding up back at her Traveller wagon in Connemara. But now Evangeline was beginning to suspect there was more to this story. That maybe Iron Feather had *summoned* her for his own reasons...

"W-what kind of magic did you have in mind?" Evangeline pressed, trying her best to keep her expression of stone and not reveal any fear.

Iron Feather picked up a large rock and held it aloft on top of his index finger, swaying his hand slightly so it wouldn't fall. "Balance magic," he replied.

"I-I don't understand what you mean." Evangeline hugged the long duster tighter around herself that Virgil had loaned her to keep warm. The fur of the buffalo hide against her neck comforted her a little.

Virgil tossed another branch onto the fire, watching the bright sparks lift into the sky and expire like fireworks. "He's talkin' about justice," he nodded as the snap and hiss of the wood died down.

Virgil dug into his pants pocket and held out a note to Evangeline. It was written in artful penmanship and addressed to presumably the owner of the next stagecoach they would rob:

You love gold more than life
and you gladly took a life to claim it.
But by the light of the moon,
nothing that shines
can protect you when it's time to pay for it.

Evangeline trembled at the words, keeping up her brave face. "What are you, Black Bart?" she said in a flat tone to hide her bewilderment. "Leaving poems after you steal from others to get some kind o' fame?"

"He don't care nothin' about money," one of the fellow outlaws sniffed. A wiry, chestnut-haired young man with sinewy muscles in his jaw and an intense gaze. "He divvies up some to us for our trouble. Then leaves the rest at the door of orphanages and charities."

Eyes wide, Evangeline twisted a little on the log she was sitting on. "I-I'm not following you—"

"Poetic justice," the blonde outlaw nodded. "Frank Topper killed our friend Caleb Lott for his claim at Destiny Creek. Then he went on to make millions in what he calls the Topper Mine. These robberies by the Bandits Hollow Gang," he shifted his gaze with reverence to Virgil, clearly a man he considered their leader, "are our way of balancing them scales. And we ain't about to stop till we give every penny to a worthy cause and bleed that son of a bitch dry."

He stared at Evangeline with a venom that was frightening —even to her. "If Iron Feather brought you here with his magic, then there must be some way for you to help. Ain't that right, Iron Feather?"

Iron Feather said nothing, but Evangeline felt as if his stare bore a hole between her eyes. "I-I don't have much experience in outlawin'," she confessed.

"You don't have to," the chestnut-haired young man pointed out. "All that's required is a certain, shall we say... dedication. At the end of each month, Topper sends his gold over to a bank in Florence. Sometimes by unmarked stagecoaches or disguised wagons, other times by narrow gauge train. He's smart as a weasel an' varies his tactics so his wealth won't be detected—"

"Or robbed," Evangeline finished his sentence, her eyes registering the plan. "An' you need me to tell you *which* coach or train it is..."

She swiped a glance at Iron Feather, who didn't nod. Her gaze appeared alarmed, as though wondering how on earth he knew of her fortune telling powers.

"Six more hits," Virgil Hollow nodded, chewing on a blade of straw. "Then we figure we'll have ol' Topper cleaned out.

Word on the street is that his vein will only last till the end o' the year. Then you can go back to wherever you came from. You in?"

Iron Feather held up his turquoise pouch, its color vibrant in the glow of the fire. Evangeline knew it held the herbs that could send her back to the present. He opened the pouch and dipped his fingers inside, pulling out a rock with a large flat section of mica imbedded in it that reflected the faces around the campfire like a mirror.

Iron Feather balanced the mica rock in one hand and the turquoise pouch in the other like a scale. "You show us Topper's gold cargos," he said, lifting up the rock, "you get the herbs." He raised the pouch even with the mirror rock.

To Evangeline's surprise, the mica in the stone acted instantly like her crystal ball at home, with images hovering over its reflective surface. But it wasn't a picture of a stagecoach or a train being robbed. The image she saw unnerved her far more than some future crime. It was a silhouette of her kissing Virgil Hollow...

"You in?" Virgil pressed, his blue eyes more tender and welled with anticipation than he probably cared to reveal, for someone who was simply looking for another member of the Bandits Hollow Gang. But under the starlight, with her face delicately highlighted by the campfire's hues, it was hard for any mortal man to resist the beauty of Evangeline Tinker.

Evangeline's gaze was arrested by Virgil's blue eyes, the same color as the medicine pouch Iron Feather held in his hand.

"I-I reckon I don't have a whole lotta choice, now do I?" she stammered. "If I'm ever fixin' to go home—"

She darted her eyes from Virgil's, focusing on the pouch for a moment. Her gaze locked on Iron Feather's to seal the deal.

"Jus' six more robberies. You promise, Indian man?"

Silent, Iron Feather's eyes glistened from the leaping flames of the fire. He tossed Evangeline the mica rock and tucked his pouch safely inside his coat pocket.

"If that's what you say," he nodded, turning to give Virgil a hint of a smile.

7

All of a sudden, the light of the campfire became hazy and dim in the antique mirror, threads of clouds obscuring the Bandits Hollow Gang from view. Frustrated, Brandi tapped insistently on the glass, to no avail. She began knocking on it like a door.

"What *happened* to her?" she demanded of Evangeline's great-great grandmother.

For a while there was a silence that Evangeline's great-great grandmother didn't attempt to fill. But then the mirror began to clear, and Brandi saw Evangeline galloping on a paint horse with its mane and tail whipping in the wind. Members of the Bandits Hollow Gang sprang from shadows along a winding, narrow road lined by steep, rocky bluffs to ambush a series of horse-drawn wagons. Evangeline held a gun in her hand, her face nearly covered with a black bandana. In her timberwolf gray eyes was nothing but defiance. Virgil couldn't help smiling at the swift way she cut off horses, while he demanded that they drop their lock boxes and open their wagon doors to unload cargos of gold.

It was clearly spring now—aspens were fringed with bright green leaves and the outlaws rode to the ambush with rolled up sleeves. Seasons began to pass, however, and soon, aspen leaves in the mirror changed to gold, or became silvery-gray and fell to the frosted ground like lost coins. Yet with every picture the mirror revealed, the Bandits Hollow Gang rode as an expert team, following Evangeline Tinker with her long, flowing hair and remarkable streak of gray as she often took the lead to halt the stagecoach or wagon horses. Months appeared to pass as they picked off overland cargos on remote mountain roads, or sometimes the Rocky Mountain Bank in Florence itself, seizing only the wealth of mine owner Frank Topper. Over time, Brandi could tell the admiration for Evangeline blossomed in Virgil's eyes, and it was with a special delight that he held her hand while laying bags of gold, cash, and bullion at the stoops of charities and orphanages after rapping on their doors.

Giggling, the two of them would dart into shadows or sometimes climb trees, their legs dangling over branches too high for anyone to see. They watched with relish as tears of joy streamed down the faces of tired workers when they opened the doors to their sudden windfalls. And every time, Virgil would clasp his palms over Evangeline's cheeks and pull her in for a kiss. Then he'd stare into her eyes as if this were his reason for living.

And each night, the mirror showed that the weary outlaws returned to Bandits Hollow, led by Iron Feather—a hiding place he told them was known only to the Ute tribe near *Tava*, their sacred mountain. He mentioned that the Utes had no love for Frank Topper and his land-grabbing ways. And there wasn't a tribe on earth that would breathe a word about the outlaws' whereabouts.

Virgil, on the other hand, *did* breathe words.

Many of them…

Brandi blushed, and her fingers clutched at her heart over the romantic way she saw Virgil take Evangeline by the hand to lay her down one night, after the other men had tied up their horses and bedded near the campfire. Virgil led Evangeline to the privacy of a cave he'd cleaned out in their hollow, flanked by boulders the size of buildings, where he'd built a small fire. Then he pulled her to the floor on the soft hides of buffalo and Native American blankets, running his fingers through her streak of gray hair and embracing her cheeks.

"Evangeline, Evangeline," he breathed onto her forehead, tenderly unfastening the pearl buttons of her velvet dress and checking her eyes to see if it was all right. "You've stolen my heart. How could I guess a wisp of a woman like you would make such a strong outlaw?"

"Strong enough to survive *you?*" she replied, flashing her gold tooth with a sassy smile that made his eyes dance. "Sometimes, I have my doubts." Then she stopped his hands from fidgeting with her buttons and held them in hers, blowing on his large fingers until they were warmed. She gently removed his gray, pinstriped shirt, with cotton soft as a child's blanket from so much wear, revealing his broad, hard chest. With a kiss to his smooth skin, she opened up her dress and laid her nakedness over his heart, listening to the beats run faster at her touch. Virgil smiled, pulling her in for a kiss and unraveling her long dress over her waist and down her hips. Soon, they'd stripped each other of their clothes entirely like armor they no longer wanted, lying together skin on skin. Evangeline traced her fingers down Virgil's muscular back and pushed his hips towards her, enveloping him with her body.

Their dance was slow at first, igniting with a fever that became overwhelming as their bodies consumed one another, making Brandi gasp and turn away from the mirror.

"Some things are too sacred to look upon," Lorraine nodded in a hushed tone. "Just wait, sweetheart, till their fire dies down."

"That don't seem possible," Brandi replied. "I fear if I look again, their desire might've burned each other to ash."

Nevertheless, after a quiet spell, Brandi dared to sneak a peek into the mirror. She saw Evangeline covered with a buffalo hide next to Virgil, gazing out the entrance of the cave at the twinkling stars. Her eyes searched for the one fixed in the sky between the treetops that shone the brightest of all: the north star.

Virgil regarded the star as well, but not with the same dreamy look in his eyes. He cleared his throat.

"Y-You ever gonna go back to your people, Evangeline?" he asked, curling a strand of her long hair between his fingers. "We only got one more hit left."

Evangeline rolled closer and snuggled her head against him, letting her hair spill over his chest like water.

"How 'bout you? You go first—"

"I ain't got no people, Evangeline. Except the Bandits Hollow Gang. You know that."

He kissed her forehead and rifled his fingers through her cascading hair. "But after the next train hit," he explained, "there ain't no vengeance to be had any more. Topper's tapped out. I've heard creditors are already after him, and some have hired a hit man to take his life. He's worth more dead than alive these days, with all them fancy houses and hotels to repossess. Reckon I'll have to figure out something else to do."

Evangeline nodded, but Virgil could tell she was swallowing a lump in her throat.

"Virgil," she pulled herself up to meet his gaze, "how does an outlaw not be an outlaw?" she whispered. "From the time the sun first shined on earth till now, t'ain't no highwayman that could ever stop. Look into my eyes, Virgil, and tell me that ain't true."

Virgil stared at her flared gray eyes like he'd been caught.

"I seen your poems all along, the ones you leave at every robbery. They're downright beautiful. But they're also lightning strikes, Virgil. Each one a bolt of electricity that puts shivers down my spine. It ain't the revenge on Topper, or the gold that thrills you. It's the chase—"

"Stay with me, Evangeline," he interrupted.

Before she could reply, he kissed her long and slow. The kind of kiss that stamped his longing on her soul, begging her to remain.

"We can ranch," Virgil promised. "Far away from here. Iron Feather knows people in Abiquiu, New Mexico. They don't ask questions down there. They've never heard of us—"

"*Everyone's* heard of us," Evangeline corrected him. "Haven't ya seen a newspaper lately? Headlines proclaim the poetic justice of the Bandits Hollow Gang from here to New York City. The whole country's rootin' for you, Virgil. You're famous—"

"Then we'll escape to another country," Virgil's eyes lit up, "like Argentina. I hear it's beautiful, an' you can take up raising cattle there. Imagine how stunning you'd look with the South American sun shinin' through your hair."

"But the law would come after us," she scolded him. "Tell me the truth, Virgil—"

Evangeline paused, reaching to her dress in a lump beside the buffalo hide and pulling out crumpled poems from her pocket. She opened up several of them, unfolding the papers to reveal their artful penmanship. Tracing her finger over the words, she pointed at lines that were love letters not to her, but to adventure. Each one reveled in their risky ambushes and daring getaways.

"If you weren't writing your poems on the chase," she whispered, "you'd cease to live, wouldn't you, Virgil? It's the love of this game that keeps ya goin'. You have no idea how much I agonize over every single robbery. Whether you'll come back to me alive—"

"But you've got your magic."

Evangeline shook her head. "Magic can't trump fate, darlin'."

She stared gravely into his eyes, her expression so stern it made him wince. But then she clutched his face and kissed him with a fierceness that surprised him, like it might be their last.

"Sooner or later, Virgil," Evangeline said, "a highwayman will always be buried by the highway. I know this for a fact, my love. That's centuries of Tinker wisdom talkin'."

"But I love you, Evangeline," he said with defiance in his eyes. "I love your strong ways, your magical talents, how the wind rifles that silver streak in your hair when you ride after a stagecoach or a train. I-I can't live without you—"

"But what if you don't live at *all?*"

"What're you saying?"

Evangeline sighed. "Each day is a toss of the dice. A gamble. I never told you about the Tinker curse—"

"What curse?"

"We drive men mad. All of 'em, for centuries." Evangeline's gray eyes searched his, and she appeared vulnerable all of a sudden, as though she feared she might fall into his pools of blue and never resurface again. "But here, Virgil, it seems like *I'm* the one who's goin' insane. I may hunger for your body in a way that sends you to the stars, but your love devours my heart."

Hesitantly, Evangeline held up her arm to him, revealing cuts on her skin. Fresh red welts from carving his name were on the inside of her forearm, with hash marks for each robbery where he didn't die, as if to shore up her faith that in the next hit he might live.

"I've gone off kilter. I think about you day an' night, worrying about whether I'll ever see you again, my thoughts spooling 'round and 'round like some crazy spinning wheel till I wish I could die. Just like all those poor men I've cursed. Maybe this is *my* poetic justice, Virgil—"

"No!" he contradicted her. He stood to his feet and gathered her slim frame in his arms, like that day she fell from the sky, and carried her out of the cave into the moonlight.

The night air was punctuated by the sounds of snoring men beside their dead campfire.

Virgil walked until they reached a ridge and a small opening in the trees, where the moonlight shone down on her face, making her appear like an angel.

"This light in your eyes won't ever fade, Evangeline. Even if I do die, don't you know I'd haunt you forever? You're my outlaw…bride."

Virgil bent down and laid her upon a bed of leaves. To her surprise, he set a bright gold nugget, as large as his fist and surely priceless, between her naked breasts.

"I been keepin' this for you. We've given thousands, maybe millions, to the needy. But my heart craves you, Evangeline. Be Mrs. Hollow?"

Evangeline studied his eyes, lit by a summer moon. "Rose Moon," she whispered, "time to reevaluate hopes n' dreams." She clutched the gold nugget that rested against her skin and rubbed it as if it were his heart. Then she linked her arms around Virgil's neck and pulled him down to her, wrapping her legs around him.

"Don't you know," she whispered in his ear, "that a Traveller's heart can only marry the moon?"

❧ 8 ❦

"**O**h my god, did she marry him?" Brandi exclaimed, pawing at the mirror that had abruptly become black. She lifted it up from the ground by its ornate, wooden frame and shook it.

"Were they gonna walk down the aisle?" Lorraine tugged on Brandi's coat sleeve, confused.

Brandi bowed her head and sighed. "Here, you hold this mirror for a second before I smash that damn glass."

As Brandi was about to pass the mirror to Lorraine, the mist reappeared, and in it she made out the form of Evangeline's great-great grandmother.

Shaking, Brandi set the mirror down against the tree, stepping back as though she feared it might bite.

From the haze, Evangeline's great-great grandmother's form became clear.

"Evangeline thought the Tinker curse couldn't affect a man from the past," she explained, "because he'd already lived his life and died over a hundred years ago, and you couldn't change history. She felt she could dally with his affection without consequences."

The woman shook her head, but then smiled a little. "Evangeline never dreamed that *she* might be the one to fall in love with her whole heart and go mad..."

Before she finished her last words, Brandi saw several riders in the moonlight along a railroad track. A wooden sign nearby said *Phantom Canyon*. From a few miles away, smoke rose from a steam engine that was advancing toward them. The Bandits Hollow Gang appeared to be waiting on this train that carried the last of Topper's gold holdings, the one he must have thought would save him from bankruptcy.

The blonde outlaw punched his buddy on the arm who rode beside him on horseback. "Watch out fer ghosts!" he cried, breaking off a stick from a nearby aspen tree to whack his friend's horse. "This canyon's been known to harbor a spook or two."

"Whaddya mean?" his buddy replied.

"Oh, 'cause it got its name from things folks see. Many a dead miner or stagecoach driver has been known to terrorize folks on this route."

"Shuttup. You're scarin' me!"

The blonde outlaw laughed and rode off, followed by his friend who didn't appear to want to be left alone.

They didn't notice that Evangeline and her horse were tucked away in the shadows behind a large boulder. As she urged her paint horse to step forward, her face became as white as the moon.

Something—or *someone*—was hovering over the railroad tracks…

Swiftly, Evangeline held up Iron Feather's mica rock like a talisman for protection. Nevertheless, the hazy likeness that appeared before her remained suspended in air. She watched as it crystallized into human form.

It was the spitting image of Virgil Hollow—

Only he'd been shot through the chest. A bloom of fresh blood stained his shirt over his heart. His features appeared sunken and pale.

Iron Feather quietly pulled his horse up beside Evangeline, startling her.

Closing her eyes for a second, she patted her chest to try and resume her breath and wrapped her fist around her saddle horn to stop her body from trembling. But then she tightened her reins and whipped out her gun from her coat pocket, holding it to his temple.

"Moon as my witness, Iron Feather," Evangeline swore, "I ain't gonna stay here an' watch the love of my life die."

She cocked the hammer, fingers shaking. Yet her gaze had a singular focus that showed she meant every word. "Hand over that turquoise pouch right now."

Iron Feather didn't budge. He remained silent in the darkness.

"It will kill Virgil if you leave," he finally whispered.

"H-He's gonna die anyway!" Evangeline burst, stumbling over her words. She pointed at the railroad tracks. "I-I saw his ghost over there, sure as I'm sittin' here breathin'. An' I bet you did, too. An' at least if I go, one of us can keep our sanity.

'Cause make no mistake about it, Iron Feather—I will *never recover* if I see Virgil Hollow die."

Evangeline pushed her revolver harder against his temple, tilting his head to the side.

"You could have shot me earlier," Iron Feather pointed out in a measured tone. Brazenly, he turned to face her, regardless of the barrel now centered on his forehead. "You could have stolen my medicine bag any night you wanted. While we slept by the campfire. But you fell in love with him, didn't you? Admit it, Evangeline—that's why you stayed."

Tears spilled down her cheeks that shined in the moonlight, dripping onto her saddle.

"Don't make me stay here, Iron Feather!" she gasped. "Don't you dare do that to my heart."

He nodded and reached into his coat for his medicine pouch.

Evangeline stared at his free hand with resignation in her eyes, as if she understood that he could've grabbed his own gun and blown her away all along, for he was a seasoned outlaw with far more years of experience behind him.

But he also knew she was right—

It would be downright cruel to make her stay.

"This medicine bag," Iron Feather said, raising it to the moon, "its color is crushed turquoise from my grandmother's necklace. The leather is the hide of my best warrior horse, *Ha'ii'ago*, who died in battle. Do not fool yourself, Evangeline. If you take this bag, its magic will track you."

"T-Track me?" Her voice fought against tremors. "What do you mean?" Evangeline snatched the bag from his hand before he could change his mind.

A piercing whistle from the oncoming train jarred her, and she took a deep breath and straightened up in her saddle. But when she turned to speak again to Iron Feather, he was gone.

In his place were a couple of white feathers marked with bands of gray on the ground. And somewhere high in the trees, an owl called, as if responding to the train's lonely whistle.

9

Exhausted, Brandi plopped herself down to sit cross-legged by the creek for a second, attempting to gather her wits. She grasped Lorraine's hand and pulled her down to sit beside her for a spell. When they nestled their long wool coats beneath their legs to keep from getting cold, Brandi cleared her throat, watching the puff of moisture escape into the frosty air.

"Granny must've made it back to the present by using an herb from that pouch," she observed in a hushed tone, fearing spirits might hear her. "And then she came to Bender Lake—"

"Where she couldn't be found," Lorraine finished her thought. "Where everyone goes to not be found. She told me that she lived in the mountains of Idaho once, but she bolted when the love of her life caught up with her."

"'Cause of the Tinker curse? She was afraid he might be crazy?"

"No," Lorraine shook her head. "From what we seen,

darlin', I'd say she skedaddled 'cause she was afraid of losin' her *own* mind. Maybe that feller warn't human. Maybe he was the ghost of Virgil Hollow——"

Brandi gripped Lorraine's arm, her heart racing.

"L-Lorraine, I saw it for myself, how the two of them up and disappeared into the creek. That's crazy talk, ain't it? Do we dare take a look at where she is now?"

Lorraine rubbed Brandi's hand, patting it kindly. "We're *family* here at Turtle Shores," she chastised. "Even though the rest o' the world thinks we're misfits. If this happened to you, you can bet we'd move heaven an' earth to get you back."

Brandi nodded with a flicker of understanding in her eyes.

"But brace yourself, honey," Lorraine warned. "Maybe Virgil Hollow really *did* go crazy, like all the others who tried to love Granny. Even as a spook."

Brandi took Lorraine's hand in hers for fortitude, giving it a gentle tug. The two women stood to their feet, and Brandi pulled her shoulders back.

"Ma'am," she called out to the mirror, "p-please show us where Evangeline is *now*."

The darkness of the mirror began to lift. All that could be seen, however, was the white reflection of the Cold Moon. Brandi sighed, fearing that perhaps the magic of this peculiar night in December might have passed. But then she saw an unusual sight in the glass.

"Lorraine, there's pretty lights, rising in the sky like fireflies!"

In the mirror, hundreds of golden lights floated toward the stars, gently ascending until they were consumed by flames.

"What are they?" Lorraine asked.

Brandi shrugged. "I ain't sure, but they look to me like luminaries. You know, those little lanterns folks put candles in for the holidays. I guess these were released to the sky. Damned if they ain't breathtaking, sweetie."

Brandi gazed with wonder at the mirror, until her eyes registered Granny Tinker in the glass, making her breath hitch.

Virgil was beside her in an outdoor patio, lighting candles to put them in delicate paper lanterns and watch them fly. He smiled boyishly at Evangeline, tracing each one with his eyes as though they were his fragile hopes.

"*Feliz navidad*," he whispered, leaning in to give her a kiss. His eyes searched hers as though they lit the flame of his heart. "What do you think of my *rancho* here in Argentina?" He raised his fingers to trace the curve of her cheek. He was older now, with silver threading his hair, but his eyes remained an earnest blue. "I built it for you. I been waiting for you, Evangeline—"

Carefully, he unbuttoned his white cotton shirt to reveal a deep brown scar on his chest, a little to the right of his heart.

"I lived that night," he breathed onto her cheek. "After the train robbery in Phantom Canyon. But I been haunted by you ever since."

Evangeline's fingers leaped to her lips. She trembled as she reached a hesitant hand to Virgil's chest, daring to press her finger against his scar.

Virgil grasped her hand suddenly and swooped in for a kiss. When he broke away, he studied her pale face in the moonlight, framed by silver hair. The platinum glow of the moon made her look younger, yet shining and eternal at the same time. "Who's the ghost now?" he whispered, kissing her forehead, her nose, her cheek before returning to her lips.

Evangeline closed her eyes and let his lips travel her face, exploring her—devouring her—until she felt him lift her body in his arms.

"Stay with me, Evangeline," he urged, carrying her to the bedroom.

"In the early twentieth century? Oh Virgil, we're a couple of ol' fools now," she said with a slip of a smile, her gold tooth glistening. "Caught in a time between times. Beneath this magic moon, how do we know what's real? And what would an ol' Traveller like me do with an outlaw in Argentina?"

"I have mines," Virgil countered. "One here in Chilecito and another in Potosi, Bolivia. Within a few more years, I'm sure they'll pay out—"

"And while you wait for that, you'll do what? Head to Chile?" she laughed. "Or don't tell me—Paraguay? All beneath the governments' noses, of course." She returned his kiss with an ardor that surprised him, but then she placed her hands on his temples and looked him in the eye. "You're still a highwayman to the core, my handsome ol' bandit. You always will be."

Virgil's eyes sparkled. "Well, you're still a Traveller. And as beautiful as they come. So that makes us perfect."

He held up the turquoise pouch he'd stolen from her in Bender Lake.

"Iron Feather's medicine bag helped me track you over the years, you know. He summoned you all along, because he wanted his friend to have someone to love, like the woman he'd loved once and buried. Someone strong enough to withstand an outlaw."

He set Evangeline gently upon a soft bed covered by brightly-colored, Argentine blankets and turned to a rustic dresser to light a candle.

"But that's just it, Virgil," she explained. "I *don't* withstand you. You drive me insane. Your outlaw love carves its way into my heart the way miners find gold. It leaves a big hole there filled with darkness whenever I'm not near you. I either worry to death about what'll happen to you. Or I worry that I'm not…"

"Not what?"

He snuggled on the bed beside her, watching her reach into the turquoise pouch and pull out Iron Feather's old chunk of rock with mica. In it, faces began to appear of all the people she had helped—and would help in the future—at Bender Lake. There was a confused teenage girl with long, curly hair, a lost tow-headed little boy, a tall young man beside him with blonde hair and bitterness in his eyes.

"I'm here on earth for a reason, Virgil, like you. To feed the ones who need it most."

Virgil glanced at the stone, but all he saw was his own reflection in the mica. "I don't know what you mean."

Evangeline sat up on her elbows and pointed to a sepia-toned photo on a mantle in the bedroom that was tucked inside a simple pine frame. It was of Iron Feather as an old man. He had on the same flat-brimmed hat, but streaks of gray ran down his long hair. He was surrounded by children who were tugging on him and smiling.

"Iron Feather didn't just bring me here to keep you an' the

Bandits Hollow Gang safe with my fortune tellin'," Evangeline explained. "Though he loves you like a brother, and would take a bullet for you."

She rolled onto Virgil's chest and gave him a sweet kiss, drawing a big heart with her finger over the bullet scar on his skin.

"He brought me here for the children, Virgil. Don't you see?" She glanced at the photo again. "The people who really needed that gold."

Virgil scanned her face, running his fingers down her cheeks and pulling her in for a long, slow kiss. It was the kiss of an old man who'd spent his life searching the whole world for what he wanted, only now pausing long enough to savor it. He tilted his head against hers.

"We fed his people," Evangeline continued, pressing her lips against his cheek for a moment. "The Ute, Apache, Navajo. Scores of children who'd been torn from their families to be raised as whites in boardin' schools. You didn't know it, but between robberies, he organized secret raids to sneak 'em out an' rode under cover of darkness to take 'em home. The government never knew. He prevailed upon me for my fortune tellin' skills to help find their parents."

Virgil's blue eyes grew wide. "W-Why didn't he tell me?"

"So if the government found out, marshals couldn't beat it out of you. Out of any of the Bandits Hollow Gang, an' get the families in trouble. He knew I came from a different time an' place—an' that I'd probably go back." A smile surfaced on Evangeline's lips. "An' I guess he suspected I was good at keepin' secrets."

"That's why he disappeared a lot," Virgil nodded with a

brooding look in his eyes. "He died poor, you know. In Abiquiu."

"He died *rich*, Virgil. Surrounded by the families an' children who loved him."

"And you? What have you been doing all these years?"

"Healing hearts. Iron Feather's work inspired me, love. That's why I headed to Bender Lake."

Virgil was quiet a long time.

He wrapped his arms around Evangeline and held her close, swallowing her in a kiss. "I know they need you," he said breathlessly as he broke away. "The brokenhearted...the lost...all the others in your Traveller world who rely on you to be their compass. But I can't go on without you." He pointed out the bedroom window at the full moon that lit their bed with a silver glow. "You are my light."

Evangeline grasped his face gently and stared into his eyes. "We're a pair, ain't we, Virgil? Two ol' outlaws, bound by what we love. You followin' your adventures, an' me followin' my heart."

A deep boom erupted outside, releasing sparks as bright as a constellation that spread a warm light over their faces. Evangeline smiled at the Christmas Eve fireworks, but then shook her head. "Maybe our magic ain't meant for this life, Virgil. It's *beyond* life. Maybe our magic is meant for the stars."

"What're you saying?" Virgil's voice had a flinty edge. "Are you leaving?"

"We can't break our hearts on one hand, steering away from what we were born to do, an' remain together, Virgil. You're an outlaw who needs to roam this world like he needs to breathe, an' I'm a Traveller who ferrets out people's secrets and stitches their hearts."

As the fireworks simmered down, an owl hooted outside.

"So that's why his people always called him Iron Feather," Virgil said softly, staring at the owl's silhouette over a branch.

"Because he was soft an' hard at the same time?" Evangeline replied. "Then that's what we'll be." She glanced up at the bird near their window with the moonlight glinting off its feathers. "Each year, under the Cold Moon, the moon in December that prophesies the renewal of what lies ahead, come to me Virgil. Keep me warm. Keep my heart alive until—"

"You die?"

She nodded. "An' I've done what I'm supposed to do. Then we can be together forever, both of us free."

"That's a long time to wait, my love." He ran his fingers down strands of her silver hair like they were silk.

"You've already waited enough. One night, one eternal night each December, when time stands out o' time, you'll be mine. Do ya hear me? All *mine*. An' I'll make love to you like there's no tomorrow. Our flame will carry us through."

She glanced at the flickering candle that spread a glow across their room.

"I'll keep following you," Virgil vowed. To anyone else, it might have sounded like a threat, but Evangeline was used to it.

"I know that," she smiled. "You found me in the mountains of Idaho, remember? An' tonight in Bender Lake."

"Spook will bring me," he insisted, nuzzling against her.

"She loves a good chase more than life itself. That old mare knows your scent by now, better than any bloodhound."

"So does the owl," Evangeline nodded. "Because Iron Feather believed in the power of love. The true kind o' love, that gives an' gives and can't never be separated by time. Will you believe that for me, Virgil?"

"I will try, Evangeline. My soul may roam this big ol' world, and maybe the next. But of one thing you can be sure —my heart finds its rest in you."

10

Brandi and Lorraine sniffed back tears beside the antique mirror poised against an old hickory tree in the snow. The glass was completely black now, finished with revealing its secrets.

"That was beautiful!" Brandi exclaimed, pulling out a hankie from her coat pocket and blowing her nose.

"I guess we can be confident he'll bring her back to us," Lorraine added. "Virgil loved her too much to take her away from her work at Turtle Shores. Helpin' folks the way Iron Feather done."

Speechless, Brandi nodded and grasped Lorraine's hand to give it a squeeze. She led her to the tree and picked up the mirror, tucking it under her arm as they headed back toward Turtle Shores.

Fortunately, there was enough moonlight left to highlight the narrow path past scraggly honeysuckle bushes to the trailer park. From a distance, Brandi spied the blinking red and green lights of her trailer that filtered through the trees. Yet as they drew closer, she noticed something out of place beside Granny Tinker's wagon.

It was a dappled-gray horse, tied by a rope to the wagon, surrounded by a man's tracks in the snow.

And the warm glow of a lantern illuminated the windows of the wagon. Tinkling laughter echoed from inside, spreading across the little glen between Bender Lake and the trailer park.

Brandi stopped, shivering in place.

"Is-Is that a g-ghost horse I'm seein', Lorraine?" Brandi tugged on Lorraine's coat. She watched the horse raise its head and nicker.

"If'n it is," Lorraine replied, trembling a little, "that mirror ought to reveal it. Lay the glass up against the wagon."

Frightened, Brandi drew a deep breath and dropped Lorraine's hand. At the count of three, she dashed to set the mirror beside the wagon, running back to Lorraine as fast as her legs could carry her. For a moment, she covered her eyes with the soft wool of her mittens, her heart pounding. When she finally dared to glance the horse's way, the only thing she could see in the mirror was the reflection of the Cold Moon staring back at them, with stars all around.

A loud clink of glasses broke the silence of the glen, as if Virgil and Evangeline were toasting the holidays with a secret stash of moonshine. Laughter pealed through the wagon, and inside, two silhouettes swayed like they were engaging in a slow, midnight waltz.

"Sounds like they're mighty happy, honey," Lorraine whispered. "May not be of this world the way a mind can grasp, but I'd say it's workin' for 'em."

"Oh Lorraine, do you think it might work for *me* someday, too?" Brandi asked, misty eyed with a tender hope in her voice. "After what I seen tonight, I don't think I'd mind if it was a spook. 'Cause a love like that might fill your soul for centuries—"

"Be careful what you wish for, darlin'," Lorraine scolded. "Remember what that lady in the mirror said—there's a price to these things. By the way, what is it?"

"What's what?" asked Brandi. She resumed her grip on Lorraine's hand and headed toward the blinking Christmas lights of the trailers at Turtle Shores.

"Well, as I recall, Granny's great-great grandma said she'd show us what happened to her after she disappeared, but only for a price. So what's our price?"

The deep call of an owl stopped them in their tracks. Silently, it flew over their heads, casting the shadow of a man with a flat-brimmed hat onto the snow.

All at once, Brandi and Lorraine appeared bewildered, turning on their heels to try and make sense of their surroundings. The owl hooted again, its echo reverberating through the woods.

"Dagnabbit!" Lorraine complained, stomping her foot. "What in tarnation are we doin' standin' out here in the snow, freezin' our butts off for?"

"I have no idea why we're here like a couple of fools in the dead of winter. I-I just can't remember." Brandi glanced up and shook her finger at the owl in a tree. "Must be that bird's dang racket," she sighed. "C'mon, Lorraine," she wrapped her arm around her friend's shoulder, "let's go to my trailer and I'll pour you some of Charlie's eggnog that I got from the Moo &

Brew." She gave Lorraine a wink. "The recipe has a little kick in it for the holidays that I think you just might like."

And as the two women trudged in the snow back to the trailer park, only the owl high up in a tree knew why they had ever been there.

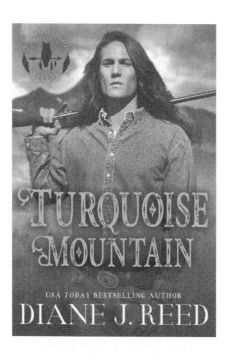

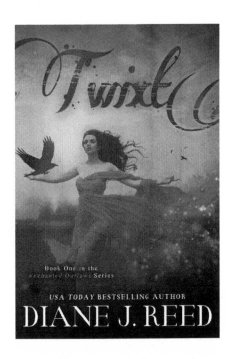

DISCOVER THE ENCHANTED OUTLAW SERIES...

He's loved her through the centuries...from ancient Ireland to the modern west.

A magical love story that will capture your heart.

Buy now!